W9-CXL-044

Armadillo's Midnight Adventure

WOODLAND MINI BOOK

To Emily Rose. — L.G.

To my sister, Annie, with love. — K.B.

Published by McGraw-Hill Children's Publishing, a Division of The McGraw-Hill Companies.

Send all inquiries to:
McGraw-Hill Children's Publishing • 8787 Orion Place • Columbus, Ohio 43240

ISBN 1-58845-460-6

1 2 3 4 5 6 7 8 9 10 CHRT 08 07 06 05 04 03 02 01

Printed in China.

Acknowledgments:
    Our very special thanks to Dr. Charles Handley of the Department of Vertebrate Zoology at the Smithsonian's National Museum of Natural History for his curatorial review.

Armadillo's Midnight Adventure

by Laura Gates Galvin   Illustrated by Katy Bratun

McGraw-Hill
Children's Publishing

As the sun melts slowly into the treetops at the end of a long summer day, an armadillo in her underground burrow wakes from a nap.

5

An odd little animal
covered in a shield of armor,
Armadillo pokes her head out
of her den, listening for danger
with her leathery ears.

Teetering on four stubby legs and dragging her long armored tail behind her, Armadillo snuffles the ground in hopes of finding some delicious bugs.

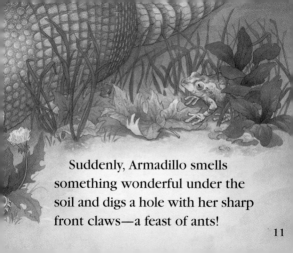

Suddenly, Armadillo smells
something wonderful under the
soil and digs a hole with her sharp
front claws—a feast of ants!

11

12

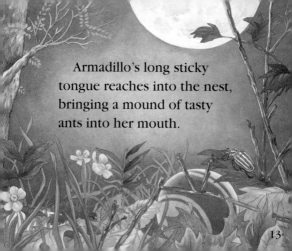

Armadillo's long sticky tongue reaches into the nest, bringing a mound of tasty ants into her mouth.

Armadillo is surprised by a coyote lurking in the shadows, and springs straight into the air, then runs away with amazing speed. The coyote jerks back in surprise.

15

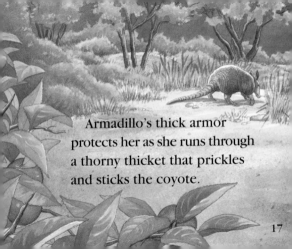

Armadillo's thick armor
protects her as she runs through
a thorny thicket that prickles
and sticks the coyote.

17

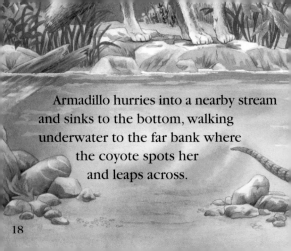

Armadillo hurries into a nearby stream
and sinks to the bottom, walking
underwater to the far bank where
the coyote spots her
and leaps across.

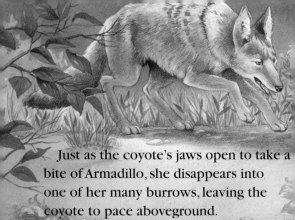

Just as the coyote's jaws open to take a bite of Armadillo, she disappears into one of her many burrows, leaving the coyote to pace aboveground.

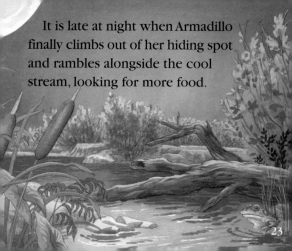

It is late at night when Armadillo finally climbs out of her hiding spot and rambles alongside the cool stream, looking for more food.

Soon, the moon disappears and Armadillo heads back to her burrow, wandering onto a road near the stream.

Armadillo tries digging into the strange, hard pavement, when a blast of air from a passing car knocks her off the road and sends her rolling back to the stream.

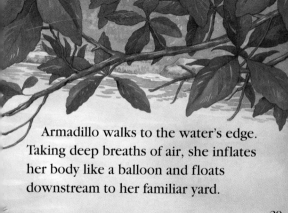

Armadillo walks to the water's edge.
Taking deep breaths of air, she inflates
her body like a balloon and floats
downstream to her familiar yard.

29

As a mockingbird greets the morning,
Armadillo's adventure comes to an end.
She settles into her soft bed of grass
for a long day's sleep.

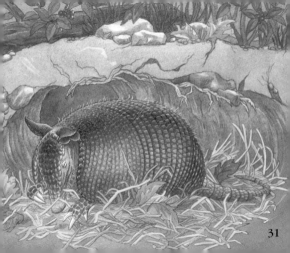

About the Nine-Banded Armadillo

Nine-banded armadillos are named for the nine movable bands in the middle of their bodies, which allow them to bend and move easily. Armadillos avoid heat and sun by sleeping in their burrows during the day and hunting at night, relying on their keen sense of smell to make up for their poor hearing and eyesight. In early spring, mother armadillos give birth to quadruplets—four identical babies—with soft leathery skin which hardens after a few weeks. This armor protects them from the teeth and claws of predators, as well as thorny plants.